For our Little Mate
~ C.W.

This edition produced 2007 for
BOOKS ARE FUN LTD
1680 Hwy 1 North, Fairfield, Iowa, IA 52556

by LITTLE TIGER PRESS
An imprint of Magi Publications
1 The Coda Centre, 189 Munster Road, London SW6 6AW
www.littletigerpress.com

Originally published in Great Britain 1997 by Little Tiger Press, London.
Text and illustrations copyright © Catherine Walters 1997
All rights reserved
ISBN 978-1-84506-681-9
Printed in China
2 4 6 8 10 9 7 5 3 1

When will it be Spring?

CATHERINE WALTERS

LITTLE TIGER PRESS

"Come inside, Alfie," said Mother Bear. "It's time
to sleep and when you wake up it will be Spring."
"When will it be Spring?" asked Alfie, "and how
will I know when it's here?"
And Mother Bear replied, "When the flowers come
out and the bees and butterflies are hovering
overhead, then it will be Spring."

So Alfie snuggled down
to sleep . . .

. . . but when he woke up
Alfie could not tell if Spring had
come or not. He tiptoed across the floor
of the cave, rubbed his bleary eyes
and saw . . .

. . . BUTTERFLIES!
"It's Spring! It's Spring!" cried Alfie.
"Wake up, Mother Bear!
Look at all the butterflies
and flowers!"

But when Mother Bear came out
she could only see the soft fall of new snow.
"Winter has hardly begun," she said.
"Go back to sleep, Alfie."
"But when *will* it be Spring?" Alfie wanted to know.
And Mother Bear mumbled sleepily, "When the
swallows arrive and the birds begin to sing,
then it will be Spring."

Then Alfie curled up
again to sleep . . .

. . . and when he woke
he was sure it must be
time for Spring.

He crept across the floor,
peered outside
and saw . . .

. . . BIRDS IN THE TREES!

"Mother Bear, wake up!" squealed Alfie.
"Spring is here! The birds are singing
in the trees."

But Mother Bear could only see icicles and hear
the wind whistling in the bare branches.
"You're dreaming, Alfie," she said.
"Now go back to sleep."
"But Mother Bear," said Alfie,
"when *will* it be Spring?"
And Mother Bear,
already half asleep, grunted,
"When the sun is bright
and the air is warm,
then it will be Spring."

So Alfie burrowed down in his
bed again . . .

and when he woke
he was quite sure Spring was here.
He padded across the floor, looked out
and saw . . .

. . . A BRIGHT SUN!
"Mother Bear, you've overslept!"
cried Alfie. "Wake up! Spring is here,
the sun's out and it's beautifully warm!"

But Mother Bear could only see
the hunters' fires and quickly
hustled him away.
"Now go to sleep!" she said.
"I will tell you when
Spring is here."

So Alfie slept and dreamed of butterflies,
birds and sunshine till something icy
touched his nose!
A tiny stream of water was trickling
through the cave.
Alfie shook his mother awake and
she growled, "For the very last time, Alfie,
it is *not* Spring."

But Alfie patted her
hopefully until she got up,
stomped through
the doorway,

and saw . . .

. . . THE SPRING!
Mother Bear rubbed her eyes and
blinked in the warm bright light.
"Spring is here after all," she smiled.
But *where* is Alfie?"